THE RUSSIAN CASE

CONNOR WHITELEY

No part of this book may be reproduced in any form or by any electronic or mechanical means. Including information storage, and retrieval systems, without written permission from the author except for the use of brief quotations in a book review.

This book is NOT legal, professional, medical, financial or any type of official advice.

Any questions about the book, rights licensing, or to contact the author, please email connorwhiteley@connorwhiteley.net

Copyright © 2023 CONNOR WHITELEY

All rights reserved.

DEDICATION

Thank you to all my readers without you I couldn't do what I love.

CHAPTER 1
7th April 2022
Canterbury, England

Private Eye Bettie English stood at her large office window and watched all the wonderful university students talk, laugh and joke with each other as they pounded the cobblestone high street.

She loved how some of them were carrying massive shopping bags from places they really couldn't afford and others were simply enjoying time with their friends.

Bettie had loved her time as a university student here in the city, she actually remembered some of the things she had bought as a student. It was even harder back then for students because whilst university was free, she didn't get all the government loans that students get now. And even now Bettie still regretted buying a little black dress from an expensive shop instead of buying some food for the week.

That had been an interesting week for sure.

Bettie was even happier now that her wonderful nephew Sean was a student. She loved how he popped in from time to time to help her with cases, but Bettie knew that looking at the students wouldn't really help her.

Bettie smelt the subtle hints of burning sage, oranges and cinnamon in the air, and whilst it managed to create a rather wonderful concoction that filled the air. Bettie just wasn't impressed with why her boyfriend Detective Graham Adams had done it.

As much as Bettie loved Graham (and she really did), she couldn't help but feel like he was taking the pregnancy a bit too seriously at this point.

Granted it was only a week or two ago that she was basically been targeted by a psychopath and kidnapped (not that she was ever in any danger), but she couldn't blame him for being worried.

Bettie rested her hands on her baby bump, put her back to the window and went over to her large wooden desk in her large office and sat down, staring into the amazing eyes of the man she loved.

Graham just smiled at her as he sat on the two chairs she had in front of the desk. Bettie had never wanted to buy expensive things for her office, but she always made sure the chairs were good enough. Not too expensive to make any clients think she was wasting her money or a target for theft, but good enough for clients to know she was very good at her job. So clients loved paying her extra money as a job well done.

What the chairs were not designed for was an amazingly hot boyfriend who had a folder of paint samples for the baby's nursery. Bettie had no idea why he wanted to start preparing it so earlier, then again, Bettie had been pregnant for four months now.

Was time running out?

More amazing hints of sage, oranges and cinnamon hit Bettie's senses, and she couldn't really deny that the smell was helping her relax more. She had little interest in the burning stuff actually helping her, but it was entertaining and pretend that Graham was being useful.

Bettie really wanted Graham to relax about being a dad. He had always been worried that he would be awful, useless and just not important in the kid's life, Bettie had tried to tell him constantly that he was going to be amazing.

That would help.

But only until the next task came along. Like creating the baby's nursery.

"What about blue?" Graham said, smiling.

Bettie just laughed. Then she realised that this was really about him wanting to find out what the baby's sex was.

They had spoken about it on a few occasions and Bettie didn't want to know, and she wanted it to be a surprise. Graham sort of wanted to know, but wasn't sure.

Most of the time they were in agreement to just wait, but the real reason Bettie didn't want to know was because she didn't know what sex she wanted.

She had no preference. She would love a baby boy because she imagined it would be like having a Sean of her own, a wonderfully caring, lovely boy.

Then again, Bettie would rather like a girl because she loved the idea of teaching her daughter about being a woman in the modern world, talking to boys and doing make-up with her. And Bettie would never admit that to anyone, being a girly-girl was the last thing Bettie ever wanted to be known as.

But if Bettie was that tempted she knew she could just talk to Sean about boys and make-up.

"Come on Bet. I love you but we need to start making a decision," Graham said.

Bettie cocked her head and as much as she wanted to frown at him. She couldn't. She loved him and all this baby stuff too much.

"Gra, we both have the day off. We have all day. Actually I have a few background checks to run for a company," Bettie said.

Graham rolled his eyes.

"Don't be like that," Bettie said.

Graham stood up and went round the desk and kissed Bettie's head.

"You've been putting this off for two weeks, Bet. Can we talk about this? Please,"

Bettie wanted to say no so badly, so she really did love him too much, Bettie almost jumped as she felt the baby kick.

Graham smiled. "I think our little one agrees

with me,"

Bettie rubbed her baby bump a little more. "You're meant to prefer me, not him,"

The baby kicked again almost in protest.

Bettie laughed and looked up at Graham. "Fine. Do me a glass of water and you a coffee. You'll talk,"

Someone knocked on the door. Graham went over, opened it and walked back in with a handful of small envelopes.

He passed them to Bettie.

Bettie rolled her eyes as she had forgotten the time of the month. The middle of the month was when all the bills got paid, including the extremely important ones. Like her Private Eye Federation Membership, her Private Eye databases memberships and Bettie's favourite the National Trust membership.

Only because Bettie loved the little gift shops.

To Bettie's surprise, all the bills were rather small compared to normal which was a massive relief, and at least she would have plenty of money left over to save, or spend or invest in whatever she fancied.

But the last letter was strange.

Bettie had never seen an envelope covered in golden foil, fancy handwriting and it even smelt. It smelt amazing of sweet oranges, cream cakes and strawberry tea. It wasn't exactly a normal letter by any stretch of the imagination.

After carefully opening it, Bettie took out a very short letter that was inviting her and a guest to London… or more specifically the Russian Tea

Rooms in the very heart of London right next to the Houses of Parliament.

Yet what really threw Bettie was the letter signed off as a personal friend. She didn't know any Russians personally and she sure as well didn't want to help any of them considering there was a war on, and she had done enough backgrounds checks in the past few days to know that everyone was on high alert for Russian agents or dodgy people.

Bettie just looked at Graham and passed him the letter, and on the very back was a cheque for forty thousand pounds with the promise of another ten thousand for going to the Russia Tea Rooms.

"We're going aren't we?" Graham asked.

Bettie smiled and got up. "We are indeed. You're a cop and if this turns out to be a Russian agent or whatever, you can arrest them,"

Graham frowned and got on his coat.

Bettie couldn't believe they were actually doing this.

Something was extremely strange about this.

But that's what excited Bettie.

Probably far more than she ever wanted to admit.

CHAPTER 2
7th April 2022
London, England

Detective Graham Adams wasn't the biggest fan of London, or Russians for that matter.

As him and Bettie walked along the narrow concrete pavement of a London road filled with immensely tall buildings with golden walls, black metal fences and horrible golden doors. Graham wasn't sure the government even allowed Russians to still be in the country.

He really didn't understand why the government allowed the Russians to live in some... expensive neighbourhoods. Graham couldn't imagine how many years he would have to work as a Police Detective to even afford a little bedroom in one of these places.

Probably a good decade or two.

But Graham wasn't a fan of London because it smelt. They might have just been walking along a road in the heart of London, but Graham could still smelt the car fumes, smoke and other trouble pollutants that no one would want to breathe in if they knew the damage it could do to them over time.

Thankfully things were improving in London, and in time Graham just hoped things would get better.

The sound of cars rushing past, people laughing and posh snobby people getting out of black unmarked cars up ahead made Graham frown.

As a police officer, he had worked with various police enforcement agencies a lot recently to stop the Russians Oligarchs from doing all sorts of things. It was awful. He had had to stop the Russians trafficking people into the UK, drugs and more recently Graham had had to stop the Oligarchs from sailing out of the country on their superyachts.

Graham hated that fact alone. He was far from hateful of people being successful, he truly believed in celebrating the success of others, but he did not believe that people needed five superyachts spread throughout the world.

Just as a gesture of contempt, Graham and some fellow officers had decided to wee all over the superyacht's control panels late one night. It was just a little gesture of protest against these rich and powerful criminals, and even if his boss found out he seriously doubted anything would happen against him.

No one liked Russians at the moment.

With the smell of sweet oranges starting to fill

the air, Graham frowned as him and Bettie stopped outside a rather wonderful hotel. Graham had to admit the hotel with its large golden windows, marble pillars on each side of the entrance and waitresses in tight uniforms looked good. But Graham knew that this place was built and run on the money stolen from innocent Russian people, and he hated that.

"Miss English?" a tall man in a waiter's outfit said in a heavy Russian accent.

Graham looked at Bettie who had changed since they left their office into a wonderful little black dress (that she had bought in university apparently), and Graham was impressed it managed to hide her baby bump quite well.

"Yes. I am-" Bettie said.

"We know who are. Bettie English and Graham Adams," the man said.

Graham and Bettie just looked at each other. Graham could see in Bettie's amazing eyes that she was concerned about all this, and he couldn't disagree. In his experience dodgy people only knew your name and what you looked like, if they had been watching you quite a while and targeting you.

Graham took a few deep breaths of the sweet orange scented air and remembered that he had called his police friends, so everyone he worked with knew where he was. Graham had little idea about how effective of a backup that would be, but it was still something.

He just hoped he didn't need it.

"Right this… way," the man said, clearly struggling to remember some English expressions.

Graham extended his arm and Bettie hooked her arm through it, and they both marched into the hotel.

To any onlookers they would simply look like a power couple.

But whatever happened Graham was going to protect her.

They were entering enemy territory.

They would be surrounded by criminals.

And that terrified Graham.

CHAPTER 3
7th April 2022
London, England

As Bettie and Graham were led to a large white square table that was easily big enough to sit 6 people, she couldn't help but smile as her excitement kept growing and growing.

Bettie was really looking forward to exploring, discovering and investigating whatever was going on here, but the Russian Tea Rooms itself was very telling about the situation.

Bettie imagined that once all the rows upon rows of large white tables were filled with Russians plotting, talking and planning to commit their various crimes against the British and Russian people. But now that was clearly not happening.

The quiet Russian opera music still played in the background to create a rather tense atmosphere, and over ten waiters and waitresses lined the marble walls waiting to be needed, but something was still missing.

Bettie had read up on Russian tea culture in the car as they drove up to London, and she had learnt enough to know that the most important thing was missing.

Where the British and most of the western world had the teapot or kettle to prepare their tea, the Russians had what was known as a Samovar. Which Bettie could only describe as a trophy shaped object with a fire in the bottom and boiling water and tea in the top part, so it was always warm.

That was missing.

And considering this place was meant to be the Russian Hub of tea culture in the UK, Bettie had been expecting there to be tens if not hundreds of them, as well as according to the internet some of the Samovars could be extremely ornate.

Bettie was expecting that here.

Yet the most telling of the state of the Russian Tea Rooms was there was only one person sitting at a table with their back to Bettie and Graham in the entire room.

Bettie knew that that was the person behind all of this and they were the person who had summoned them. As she got closer, Bettie noticed the table the woman was sitting at was very neat. Too neat.

The table didn't have too much on it. It had three tea cups, a miniature Samovar (Bettie didn't know they existed) and a platter of sorts. Bettie wasn't sure what the platter contained but there were little bowls of was looked like jam, custard and other sweet treats.

Bettie rubbed her baby bump gently as she realised that the Russian woman probably didn't know she couldn't smell animal products or she would vomit. One of the stranger effects of her pregnancy.

Bettie and Graham went to the table and a pair of waiters pulled them out a warm chair, and they both sat down.

Bettie was immediately hit with the wonderful senses of strawberry, apricot and raspberry jam. Some of her favourites, and there were even hints of custard in the air.

It was strange how Bettie wasn't wanting to gag or vomit at the smell. She realised that for some reason they a had little bowl of custard on the palate that was vegan, and that alarmed her.

First the Russian woman knew where Bettie and Graham lived, what they looked like and now she knew about Bettie's reaction to animal products. Whoever this woman was, she knew way too much.

Bettie finished getting comfortable and looked at the Russian woman. Even with the foundation, lipstick and dyed brown hair, Bettie would always recognise that woman.

She honestly couldn't believe that she was staring at Penelope Bishop, or whatever her true name was. Bettie had met her once on an adultery case two Christmases ago and it turned out she was a Russian hoping to invest in the client's company but he had rejected Penelope and whoever else she worked for.

Penelope had promised to kill him and Bettie's client would get extremely rich. Bettie didn't want to believe it was true at the time.

But on the 2nd January 2021, his car had been driving down the motorway, he was speeding and crashed. Then Bettie's former client got extremely rich indeed.

Bettie's felt her company tense as she realised something very critical about that last encounter. Since Bettie never thought she would see the Russian again, Bettie promised to do a single case for her in exchange for Penelope not going after her client now she had control of the company.

Bettie feared the Russian was going to collect on that promise.

"I told you I would find out who you were Miss Bettie English," the woman said.

Bettie smiled. She was quickly realising how determined and resourceful she was.

"What name are you going by these days?" Bettie asked.

"We'll stick with Penelope Bishop today my dear," Penelope said.

Graham clicked his fingers as he remembered where he recognised her from.

"Why did you call us?" Bettie asked.

Penelope picked up at the mini-samovar and poured the three of them some amazing smelling black tea. Then she mixed in a spoonful of strawberry jam. Bettie was rather interested in how the Russians had tea.

"Relax Miss English, this is all vegan. I would never endanger a baby and its mother,"

Graham snorted. Bettie smiled.

Penelope rolled her eyes. "I know what you're thinking. Ironic statement coming from a woman who's government is bombing civilians,"

Bettie tipped her head forward.

"I understand you both," Penelope said, frowning at Graham.

Bettie quickly looked at Graham and he looked really puzzled.

"I did some research on your aliases," Bettie said, "Is it true you have a Russian father, English mother and you were raised here?"

Bettie smiled as she saw the flashes of shock and horror on Penelope's face.

"Um yes. This should explain to your boyfriend why I speak like your people. But I think I would have preferred growing up in Russia. This country is so… unremarkable,"

Bettie placed her hand on Graham's hand.

Then Bettie grabbed a spoon and took a heaped teaspoon of custard and mixed it into her tea. This was going to be amazing.

"Why are we here?" Bettie asked.

Penelope rolled her eyes. "It should come as no surprise to you my friends have all had their assets sanctioned by your weak government,"

Bettie nodded.

"My friends have all had to move money, assets and people out of the UK, Europe and the US,"

"And yet you remain?" Graham asked.

Penelope took a long sip of her tea. "Well yes. There is a reason for that. Thankfully, your government is wonderfully weak against us. For example, all my shell companies have 12 months to reveal who actually owns them,"

"And you plan to move everything in that time," Bettie said, coldly.

Penelope nodded and raised her teacup in a mocking cheers.

Bettie listened to Graham mutter something and she didn't want to even think about what Graham was experiencing. He was a cop, a very good one, so all this talk about breaking and bending the laws must have been torture to him.

"Your government has given me enough time to sort myself out, and as I have no ties to our glorious President I doubt I'll be sanctioned,"

Bettie nodded and smiled as she believed she was starting to see the entire point of this. This wasn't a case per se, this was a mission to gloat and prove to Bettie how great Penelope had become since their last encounter.

But there was something off.

"Wait, only Oligarchs can be sanctioned. You weren't one last time we met. You said you were playing with money of others," Bettie said.

"Aye my dearest Bettie. It's amazing what influencing elections, companies and other ties for my wonderful government can do to a woman's reputation,"

Graham took up and went for his handcuffs.

"Sit back down!" Penelope shouted.

The waiters and waitresses moved closer.

Bettie grabbed his arm and forced him back down.

"I doubt my government would never allow you to arrest me," Penelope said, "but I bought you here for a very special reason,"

Bettie felt her stomach tense even more. She knew this was going to be bad.

Penelope raised her teacup high in the air. "I want you to commit treason for me,"

CHAPTER 4
7th April 2022
London, England

Graham hated all of this Russian stuff. It was flat out stupid how the Russians how tea, everyone knew tea had to be made in a teapot and a kettle. None of this stupid samo-ar rubbish, everyone should have used a kettle!

And as for this putting custard, jam and other things in tea. That was outrageous. Tea should always be drunk as tea with milk or sugar, none of this other flavour rubbish that stripped away the amazing flavour of real tea.

Graham hated the Russians.

Even this tea room was an abomination with its marble walls, rows upon rows of white tables and waiters and waitresses lining the walls. This was all so Russian, it was just typical for those people to try to have all the might and power, but it was just pathetic in reality.

All this was, was a power play and something meant to intimidate him and Bettie. Graham wasn't having any of it, and he really didn't like the smell of the room.

The tea room might have smelt good with the smell of the strawberry, apricot and raspberry jam, but it was all so unneeded. Graham didn't expect anything less from Russians.

And now this outrageous woman who was clearly a criminal and someone who supported her atrocious government was asking them to commit treason on behalf of Russia.

Graham was never ever going to do that, and Bettie wasn't either.

The moment he got back to Canterbury and his police station he was going to report Penelope Bishop and get her sanctioned. He was never having a Russian that was threatening the UK in the country he loved.

"If you two are done being shocked, can I explain?" Penelope said.

Bettie slowly nodded. Graham just wanted to leave, there was nothing this woman could say that would change his mind.

"As you know I am extremely good at influencing events for the Glory of Mother Russia. I can change election results, referendum results. That UK one was fun to do. And I can influence companies,"

The first time she mentioned it Graham hadn't

realised what it meant, but now she was emphasising it. It finally clicked what she was talking about, because these days if you wanted to truly destroy an economy, all you need to do is get the major international firms to pull out of a country. Especially the payment providers.

"What business are you after?" Graham asked.

Penelope grinned. "What do you know of CryptoMill?"

Graham and Bettie just looked at each other and laughed. It was a little start-up company in London that had approached Bettie to be on retainer with the company for any investigating they needed doing.

But Bettie had denied them the contract. It turned out that the company was nowhere near as eco-friendly as they claimed, and their online safety checks to make them comply with anti-money laundering laws and other similar laws were as fake as anything.

"We know them," Bettie said.

"We don't like them," Graham said, firmly.

Penelope poured herself another cup of tea using that stupid mini-samo-whatever.

"That is excellent news. Because I believe they are a threat to the west and the sanctions your governments are imposing on my Glorious Leader,"

Graham just cocked his head. This made no sense why Penelope would be wanting to help them and their governments sanction the Russians. It made no sense whatsoever, and why did she call them and not the security services?

"Why?" Bettie asked, carefully.

"Because my dears, CryptoMill is planning to open up operations in Russia. This would allow non-Russia money to flow into Russia and support the economy and the President's war machine,"

"A president you support," Graham said.

"Mr Adams," Penelope said, "in these trying times, we must do what we can for our countries. I am giving you a company that seeks to destroy all the work your government and allies have done,"

Graham wasn't buying it. There had to be another angle here, he wasn't even sure if what she was saying was true.

Penelope finished her tea and stood up. "If you two do not believe me, that is fine. Keep my fifty thousand pound check,"

Then a waiter came over with another cheque and Penelope gave it to Bettie.

"Here my dear, here is the ten thousand,"

Bettie carefully placed it in her pocket and cocked her head. "Why? Why you trying to get rid of your money?"

Graham nodded. That was a good question.

"Because my dearest Miss English, I know your boyfriend will go back to the police and report me. Giving this alias about a month before Penelope Bishop is sanctioned. So I have a month to play with my assets and create a new… ID as you English say,"

Graham just wanted to punch this woman. She

clearly knew every single loophole in the system, the system he loved and wanted to protect.

But he'd be lying if he wasn't at least a bit interested in this CryptoMill company.

Graham waved his hands to grab her attention. "I will report you. But what do you have on this company?"

Penelope shrugged. "I don't. But if I did, I would start with a recent accident that made the co-founder become cold and is no longer... there isn't a good translation. Dead is what you people call it,"

Then Graham watched Bettie eat spoonfuls of the jams and custards and drink the tea before they were escorted out of the building.

And as much as Graham hated that Penelope Bishop.

If there was a threat to his country, people he loved and most importantly beautiful Bettie.

Then Graham was going to investigate.

No matter how much he hated Russians.

CHAPTER 5
7th April 2022
Canterbury, England

Back at her wooden desk in her office, Bettie was on her laptop researching the company that Penelope Bishop had given them. Bettie hated how this was all so secretive and she was actually starting to fill like a traitor in some way.

Even if CryptoMill was a company that was seeking to help the Russians escape the western sanctions, Bettie still felt like this was a matter for the police, security services and the government.

And that is what bothered her so much.

The amazing smell of freshly baked bread, sweet fluffy cakes and rich creamy vegan hot chocolate filled the office through the open window from the busy high street below. Bettie was definitely going to make sure Graham got her some treats later on.

But the entire thing still bothered Bettie, Penelope could have told anyone about this company.

She could have contacted the government, MI5 and any similar organisation that could investigate and stop the company.

She didn't though.

Instead Penelope had hunted Bettie and asked her for help. Even the word *help* might have been a little strong, Bettie had no doubts about the power, resources and influence of Penelope. That only added to the strangeness of it all.

So Bettie's current plan was to let Graham continue to go down to the police station, open up an official investigation, all whilst Bettie worked on things her end.

She always loved how Private Eyes could do more than police officers in certain situations, and given what the threat of CryptoMill meant to national security, she was going to use that.

Even though Bettie dropped out of International Relations at university, she still monitored the news enough to know if CryptoMill managed to help people send money into Russia, support the Russian economy then there would be nothing stopping the Russian Government from continuing to attack innocent countries.

And sooner or later, Bettie knew for a fact that they would attack the UK if they weren't stopped. Bettie didn't even want to think about what that would mean her own family, her wonderful nephew Sean and her own soon-to-be-born baby.

Bettie had to stop this no matter what.

The laptop buzzed as it finished running CryptoMill through the various databases that Private Eyes had access to, and Bettie was shocked to say the least.

When she had investigated the company before, Bettie had found tons of little details that made her conclude that the company had seriously lied to its investors, the government and the police. Since the company didn't comply with anti-corruption, money laundering and other laws that were designed to harm criminal empires.

CryptoMill was a criminal empire now.

Bettie had never seen so many dodgy bank transactions. It seemed like they weren't even trying to hide their criminal intentions anymore, known criminal gangs were transferring thousands of pounds to the company. Only for the company to transfer it seconds later to oversea bank accounts.

It was perfect really.

As much as Bettie loved the police and other law enforcement agencies, they were understaffed and very underpaid, so they only focused on the obvious things if the target wasn't big enough. The agencies probably watched the criminal gangs "invest" in CryptoMill and didn't check to see where the company was sending that criminal money.

It was clever. Too clever.

Bettie was even impressed with the business as a whole, they already knew how to lie. Bettie simply explained Cryptocurrency as digital money that was more secure than the internet and easier to trace.

It was an extreme simplification but it had always worked for Bettie.

After a few swipes of her laptop, Bettie managed to see that most of the cryptocurrency in the company belonged to the Co-founder (or now just Founder) a Mrs Jade Fox.

According to the research Bettie could find on her, Jade Fox was your normal everyday tech person. She studied at university in London, she developed her own Cryptocurrency at the age of 20 and she was a very clever woman.

And every newspaper article, university column and business website all said how wonderful she was. They all made her out to be this saint who was going to transform the world.

But the strangest thing was there was no mention of international expansion. Jade Fox only operated in the European Union, the UK and the USA. There was no mention of Russia.

Of course, Bettie knew it would be stupid for her to mention it in case the security services targeted her, but in all of Bettie's experiences tech people were offer arrogant enough to try and hint at their criminal activities.

There was no such hinting here.

Knowing that this was all she was going to get out of the databases and accounting records, Bettie realised she had to actually go and speak to Jade Fox and investigate the company in person.

So first thing tomorrow morning Bettie and Graham were going to have to go to London.

CHAPTER 6
8th April 2022
London, England

As Graham and Bettie went into a large glass Foyer in a high-rise block of offices in the heart of London, Graham was a little surprised at how ugly the Foyer was. He would have expected it all to be clear glass with comfortable seats and even a few fake plants.

The reality was nothing like that.

Instead the Foyer was nothing more than a patch of marble flooring with a front desk on the far side of it. The only thing the Foyer had going for it was the bright sunlight coming through the glass walls.

The sound of journalists talking, taking pictures and arguing filled the Foyer as Graham and Bettie stuck to the back of the crowd.

Graham was more than impressed with some of the equipment they had. Then he started to notice that some of the journalists here were the best in the country, Europe and the world. It was impressive.

Apparently Bettie had found out last night there was meant to be a massive speech today from Jade Fox about some new technology and deals going on. Bettie had guessed CryptoMill was going to announce it was entering on the London Stock Exchange, but Graham doubted it.

For a company to go on the Stock Exchange, it had to be trading millions of pounds and be invited for the most part. Graham doubted the company had that sort of power, but judging by the types of journalists here, he was actually starting to regret that idea.

The heat everyone was giving off was immense, and Graham made sure he held Bettie's hand in case it got too hot for her. Just because they were investigating a company with potential national security concerns doesn't mean he wasn't going to put his partner first.

"Tell me again what the Chief said," Bettie said quietly.

Graham smiled. "Thankfully, the Chief of Kent Police has signed off on our own private investigation. Everyone in policing is concerned about Russian agents in the police, so we're keeping this very quiet,"

"And now you two know why I didn't go to them," Penelope said as she stood next to Graham.

Graham just laughed. This was exactly the sort of clever move he had been expecting, he was just concerned about how many more times was she going to pop up.

"I presume," Penelope said, "that your Home Office is aware of your investigation,"

Graham nodded. The Home Office was in charge of all domestic security issues so his police Chief did need to notify them and get them to sign off. Thankfully the Chief had managed to get it signed off by the Home Secretary himself, so only he could to see it.

"Why are you here?" Bettie asked.

"Now, now Miss English. I am a free citizen, I can do what I pleased and I think we are about to get a shock," Penelope said pointing forward.

Graham focused on the front of the Foyer and frowned as he saw Jade Fox. She didn't exactly look like a crazy criminal tech person with her long black dress, golden necklace and pretty face. But he had been surprised before.

He couldn't drop his guard.

When she stopped in front of all the journalists, she posed for a few photos and Graham felt a bit unnerved by her. It was like the entire crowd was captivated by her and her looks and her smooth movements.

After a few photos were taken, Jade waved her hand and everyone fell silent and focused on her.

"Hello everyone," Jade said, smiling. "Today I am not going to do any dramatic speeches. I will not ask for investors or anything else,"

Graham felt his stomach tighten and he gripped Bettie's hand tighter.

"Instead I would like," Jade said, "to announce Crypto is entering the London Stock Exchange in a couple of minutes and I have some even more exciting news that will help us to transform the world,"

Graham wished he could just arrest her now. He just knew exactly what she was going to say.

"The world is changing," Jade said. "Countries are being attacked and isolated like never before. Innocent Russian people are suffering because of the actions of their government. We say no more,"

There was a massive gasp in the room.

"So we will be expanding the CryptoMill network into Asia in two days and we will allow innocent Russian people to get money in from the outside world. It is not fair that they suffer and starve because of the actions of their Criminal Government,"

Graham gasped again. Knowing it could happen and actually hearing it confirmed was something else. This was horrific.

"Any questions," Jade asked.

Graham had been expected the entire room to explode with questions from journalists, but there were none. Everyone was too stunned.

Bettie raised her hand. "How will you make sure the Russian government or their war machine doesn't get a hold of this money?"

Jade smiled. "Thank you Miss English. We are a

cryptocurrency company so it is very secure. If I transfer money to you, then only you can spend it. No government can hack an account and take it out. That money belongs to you only,"

Bettie nodded and then everyone else started asking questions.

Graham and Bettie looked at Penelope.

"Before you both ask," Penelope said. "No I did not know this would happen in this fashion. The dead co-founder contacted me about a possible move, but then he died. I could seriously focus on that, but believe me when I say this… something else is going on,"

Graham shook his head. This wasn't right. It was outrageous CryptoMill would try to do this, they might believe they were helping the Russian people but Graham knew for a fact it was only a matter of time until the criminal government learnt how to hijack the system and protect themselves.

Bettie nodded. "What is going on?"

Penelope shrugged. "I… I don't know. All I know is the Co-founder said there was something in this computer system that would completely invalidate the Western Sanctions against my country,"

"Why do you care?" Graham snapped.

Penelope gave him a devilish smile. "Because my dearest Englishman, there are plenty of opportunities in the Motherland during times of strike. If your pathetic governments keep playing along, it creates more opportunities for me, and you never ever know

I might end up in the President's Glorious Inner Circle,"

Graham and Bettie just smiled and shook their heads as they watched Penelope walk away.

Graham knew she was a cunning scheming little woman.

He was actually starting to respect her.

But now this was a lot bigger than some company wanting to break the law.

This was a threat to everyone Graham loved.

But he still didn't know how this would affect him in the long term.

He had no idea at all.

CHAPTER 7
8th April 2022
London, England

It turned out after a quick google search and a reading good news agency, Bettie found out that if Russia invalidated the western sanctions then there was nothing except war that would stop them and their war machine.

Bettie wasn't having a war started if she could help it. And she was going to damn well try.

With Graham having to go outside for a phone call with the Kent Police Chief, the Home Sectary and someone from MI5, Bettie went into the hot crowd of shocked journalists to try and get more information.

The Foyer was nothing special and Bettie was a bit disappointed that the only thing that welcomed visitors when they first entered the building was a marble and glass, but at least the wonderful sunlight shining bright through the glass walls added a touch of warmth to the place.

But even that seemed to be dimming.

Bettie still wasn't impressed with Penelope. She should have been plain with them from the start, but at least she now knew everything Penelope knew. And as much as Graham didn't trust her, Bettie was starting to understand that Penelope wanted to exploit the war as much as she could.

It was evil and Bettie was determined to stop her, yet she understood it too. From what she knew about Russia, women were still treated with no respect or equality, so only strong, rich, powerful women got any sort of respect Bettie enjoyed on a daily basis (even if that respect was lacking in some places), so Bettie understood why Penelope had to exploit situations to gain power.

It was still wrong though, and Bettie had to stop her.

A few steps away from her was a short little woman in a posh flowery dress and she and her cameraman were muttering about something. Something about a problem with the camera.

Bettie went over to them. "I'm sorry to overhear, but are you okay?"

The little woman smiled. "Miss English, right? Maya Jean, BGD News,"

Bettie smiled and shook her head. "Before you asked, Jade knows me because she wanted me to work for her,"

Bettie wanted to say more but she had a feeling

that revealing too much about how dodgy the company was wouldn't help her investigation.

Maya cocked her head. "Turn off the recorder,"

The cameraman rolled his eyes and did what she said.

"Miss English? Thee Bettie English,"

Bettie smiled and nodded. She didn't know she was known to the media.

"Oh wow," Maya said. "Um, I covered some your cases for my channel. Impressive stuff. But you wouldn't be here unless... what's going on?"

Bettie bit her lip. She didn't think that any of these media people would be any use to her, but now she was talking to Maya, she couldn't help but feel like she had more allies than she realised. And BGD News wasn't exactly a small news agency, it was actually the size of the BBC and Sky News.

Potentially some powerful friends.

"You know," Bettie said, "I'll make you a deal. Give me your phone number and you tell me about the Co-founder's death and I'll make sure *you* get the exclusive story,"

Bettie wondered if Maya was going to explode from excitement. She was jumping up and down in the air so much.

Maya passed her phone number over to her. "Well Bettie, the Co-Founder was called Finn Ellis and he was Jade's first boyfriend at university. They formed the company together and everything, but there was a massive falling out,"

Bettie nodded.

"A source told me that the fight was over the direction of the business. Jade wanted the business to become the next superpower that could overpower governments and control the world,"

Bettie frowned. It might have sounded silly but given the amount of the Anti-trust lawsuits that were floating around in other countries because companies had gotten bigger and more powerful than various governments, she wouldn't be surprised if that was true.

"What did Finn want?" Bettie asked.

Maya stepped closer. "He wanted to keep the business smaller for now. He would have vetoed the decision to make the company public and go on the Stock Exchange,"

Bettie looked at the floor. It was starting to become clearer that this was probably no accident, in her experience whenever two founding members had polar opposite views of the business only two things could happen. The two people could compromise, or one could disappear.

"What about the accident itself?" Bettie asked.

Maya shrugged. "No one really knows too much about it. There was only one News agency allowed to interview the staff and create the reports about it. We all got the reports from them,"

Bettie could understand that, but it was still strange.

"What company was it? And what happened?"

Maya titled her head slightly. "Russian Empire News was the channel, and apparently Finn was driving down the motorway outside London. He was speeding and crashed,"

"And you don't find that a little odd?" Bettie asked.

The cameraman laughed. "Yo Bettie. Anything Russian Empire News does is dodgy. Come on May, Jade looks free now,"

Bettie nodded her goodbyes and thanks to Maya and watched them walking towards Jade. Even after answering so many questions, Jade still looked in complete control and like she had an answer for everything.

But that accident with the Co-founder sounded stranger than she wanted to admit, if there wasn't a massive falling out between the company founders beforehand, Bettie never would have thought of it as suspicious. But they had had a falling out.

And that really troubled Bettie.

Then if she added the falling out to the warning Finn sent Penelope. Things just weren't adding up so Bettie decided there was only one thing left for her to do.

She needed to see the car Finn Ellis died in.

And she needed Graham and the police for that.

They needed to go to the Car impound.

CHAPTER 8
8th April 2022
London, England

Graham might have loved Bettie but she demanded the world!

Graham didn't have the heart to tell her how much paperwork, promises and other stuff it had taken for the Met police to give him and Bettie access to the car that Finn Ellis died in.

Thankfully as him, Bettie and Senior Forensic Specialist Zoey Quill with her forensic bag (who that amazingly come up from Canterbury to help out) stood in a fenced off car garage in the east of London. Graham couldn't believe how hot it was, he could feel the sweat rolling down his back.

At least Graham could see that beautiful Bettie was okay in her jeans, white blouse and boots that still managed to hide her baby bump well enough. Graham almost felt underdressed when he focused on Zoey's long white summer dress that he had never seen before.

He normally only saw Zoey in a white lab coat, but it was good to have her out in the field with them.

The sound of a car slowly driving towards them made all three of them smile, Graham waved to the driver as a large blue Ford Fiesta drove towards them.

Graham had seen a lot of car accidents in his early years as a cop but he had never seen a car look so good after an accident. It was still clear from the smashed headlight and bumper that a crash had occurred but he couldn't see any damage to the windscreen, side or hood of the car.

The car stopped and a tall man in a blue jumpsuit hopped out and threw the keys at Graham. He smiled and thanked him then the three of them were left alone.

"See anything special Zoe," Bettie said.

Graham left out a deep breath of the horrible London air, he was more than grateful that Zoey and Bettie were getting along.

"I've seen drunk driving incidents in worse conditions than this," Zoey said.

Graham couldn't disagree. If he had seen this car in the "wild", the only thing he could have thought had happened was the car had bumped into a lamp post. He never would have believed the car was speeding down a motorway and crashed.

"What do you think the speed of the car was travelling at?" Graham asked Zoey.

She shrugged. "The car wasn't speeding on a

motorway. I can tell you that much,"

Graham nodded and opened the car's passenger door. The car stunk of... bleach and other harsh cleaners, he waved Bettie away just in case the chemicals would make her sick or even worse, hurt her or the baby.

Zoey tapped his shoulder and Graham went round the car and got in the front driver's side.

But when he sat down in the car and watched Zoey connect her tablet into the car's electronic systems, he was surprised to see how wrong the mirrors were. Graham had read the police report of the accident and noticed how Finn Ellis was about his height.

There was no chance Graham would drive a car like this, and there was absolutely no reason for the police officers to change the mirrors as they were literally driving it onto a lorry for transport and parking it.

So the only conclusion Graham could draw was someone else had been driving the car on the motorway and judging by the way the mirrors had been positioned, it was someone a lot shorter.

"Found something," Bettie said.

"What?" Graham asked, not wanting to get out of the car.

"The broken headlights. They were smashed with something metal. I can see metal shavings amongst the glass,"

"Bag it please!" Zoey shouted.

Bettie nodded and went over to Zoey's forensic bag.

This was just becoming curiouser and curiouser. It was clear as day someone had messed with the car. First the mirrors, then the headlights and Graham was sure Zoey was going to find something.

"The mirrors aren't right too," Graham said. "They're positioned for a shorter person,"

Bettie shook her head as she collected some of the samples.

"What about you Zoe?" Graham asked.

Zoey huffed a few times. "I'm connected to the car's systems,"

Graham nodded. That sounded good.

"But I can't find anything. No GPS, no record of when the car was used. Even the car turning on for the person to drive it to us isn't there,"

"Is that strange?" Graham asked.

Zoey laughed. "Yes. Basically any car made after 2010 is a hack waiting to happen. All cars nowadays are massive computers and they record everything,"

"Gra," Bettie said, "how did the police know he was speeding?"

Graham opened his mouth but he couldn't remember. Come to think of it, he didn't think the report mentioned that explicitly, the report just assumed that the reader knew he was speeding.

That alone was strange.

Graham's phone went.

"Wow!" Graham shouted, as his phone opened

up on the stock price for CryptoMill.

"What babe?" Bettie asked.

"Guess the stock price for the company,"

Zoey shrugged. "Ten pounds,"

Graham shook his head.

"Two hundred," Bettie said.

"Five thousand pounds a share," Graham said.

All three of their mouths dropped and then they all just looked at each other. Graham completely agreed that was strange, considering how anti-Russia the world was at the moment Graham would have believed the stock price to crash.

But it was only growing with each passing hour. It had only been four hours since Jade Fox's announcement and each hour the stock price had been doubling.

"I think we need to look at who's investing," Bettie said.

Graham nodded.

"You might want to look at this first," Zoey said, getting out of the car.

Graham did the same and the three of them stood together in a little circle.

"On the day of the massive falling out between the Co-Founders something was installed in the car. I don't know what it was because seconds after the accident occurred. It executed itself. There are no traces of it," Zoey said.

"Then how do you know it was there?" Graham asked.

"Because," Zoey said, "my tablet shows me there was an energy spike in the car and that is typical of the car needing more energy to run another program. It's like if you plug in a Sat Nav, some of your car battery goes to powering that,"

Graham nodded. That was a great analogy.

Graham and Bettie just stared at the car. They had strange mirrors, smashed up headlights and a strange computer virus that erased the car's computers.

Something massive was going on here.

And that was before they considered the stock price.

Considering Russians, tech companies and national security was at play here.

Graham was utterly terrified of failing.

Failure wasn't an option.

CHAPTER 9
8th April 2022
London, England

As Bettie sat around a large fake-wooden conference table in a London police station with glass walls around her, she had put her feet up on the chair next to her and stared at her laptop as she tried to piece together what on earth was going on.

It was extremely strange how the accident had been so clearly faked and yet no one had even detected it in the police. At first Bettie wouldn't have been surprised in some Russian had influenced or even infiltrated the police, but Bettie was starting to wonder if that would be far, far too easy.

So far there was so little evidence that the police had been involved in the first place, even some of the most basic police procedures were followed according to Graham, so Bettie had to wonder if the police were given the accident later on.

The amazing smell of rich creamy coffee started

to filter through into the conference room and Bettie was flat jealous of all the cops outside. They all got to enjoy coffee, cakes and all the other things that pregnant women shouldn't have. Bettie was really starting to miss coffee.

After a few more deep breaths of the amazing creamy stuff, Bettie started to feel a bit sick and then she realised that the cream the cops were using had to come from a cow.

Bettie looked up at the ceiling and rolled her eyes as she saw there was a large air-conditioning grill in the ceiling and that was pumping in fresh creamy coffee tainted air.

Bettie wasn't impressed.

She forced herself not to gag or focus on the smell until Graham got back and he could turn it off for her.

Out of everything that was going on, Bettie wanted to focus on the Stock Exchange and what was happening there. After dating a boy doing accounting at university (he was probably the most boring boyfriend she had ever had), Bettie had managed to learn a lot about Stock investments.

And there were three main ways how a Stock price increase, and given how the company's stock had doubled every hour. They had to be using some very extreme methods.

The first thing was arguably the most innocent. A stock price increased because a company was selling more products so the business value was increasing.

Bettie wasn't sure if that was happening in this case, because as far as she could tell CryptoMill wasn't making any more sales or making more money. It was strange.

Then Bettie remembered that the increase to a business' value didn't need to be real for stock prices to increase. Investors only needed to believe the business would increase in value.

And knowing how much Jade Fox was lying to her investors already, Bettie fully believed Jade was capable of manipulating investors even more.

A massive hint of the creamy-coffee-scented air invaded the conference room as sexy Graham came in and sat on the chair where Bettie was resting her feet, and she explained how the business value increasing increased the stock price.

"What about the other two ways?" Graham asked.

Bettie moved around a little bit to get more comfortable. "It could simply be the momentum of which people are buying them,"

"How does that work?" Graham asked.

"Quite simply," Bettie said, "CryptoMill at the moment is a runaway train of money. There is so much money on the train that it keeps going faster and faster and faster,"

"And other investors want to jump on the train to make more money," Graham said.

"Yes," Bettie said. "Like if the stock price was £5,000 when we bought it. We would want to jump the train sooner rather than later so we could add to the momentum and maybe increase the stock price to £10,000 before it slowed down,"

Bettie shook her head at that idea. It still didn't feel right to her.

"But you don't believe that's what's going on?" Graham asked.

Bettie sort of shook her head. "It is definitely going on to some extent. I just don't think it's the main factor and I doubt it would explain the stock price doubling every hour,"

"Then what?"

Bettie smiled. "I think the CryptoMill is buying its own shares,"

Graham's eyebrows rose. "How would that help them?"

Bettie stood up and struggled to contain her excitement. It really was rather brilliant.

"Right Graham. When a company goes public on the stock exchange they give out a set number of shares. Let's say the company offered 100,000 shares in the company,"

Graham nodded.

"Then after the first few waves of investing, that number might decrease to 90,000 but that doesn't help you if you want to make quick money,"

Graham smiled. Bettie loved how he was starting to guess where this was going.

"So the company buys so much shares to make them rarer. And because these stock shares are a lot rarer, it increases their value,"

Graham stood up and paced round the table for a moment.

"What if all three of those factors happened and someone did a variation on the last one?"

Bettie cocked her head. She wasn't sure what he meant.

"What if one investor was buying up stock that would make it rarer? Both the company and a secret investor was buying up most of the stock," Graham said with a smile.

Bettie went to ask another question but then she realised who this mystery investor was.

"Come on Graham. I doubt Penelope would invest her own money in the company,"

"I agree, but what did you tell me when we first met her those two Christmases ago?"

Bettie smiled. "That she played with the money of others. You think she contacted her Oligarch friends and got them to give her their money for safe keeping so they wouldn't be sanctioned by the West,"

Graham nodded.

"And because we think she wants to do a power play," Bettie said. "I think we'll find the Russians who gave Penelope that money will very soon lose it,"

"Is that why she wants us to take down this company?" Graham asked.

Bettie shrugged. "It's perfect really. A Co-Founder warns you about a threat to her plans. Penelope sees it as an opportunity to invest in the company and waste the money of her enemies,"

"Making them broke and desperate for Penelope to save them probably. She would still have her own money,"

Bettie laughed. "Meaning all these Russians that Penelope lost their money, ask her for more to sustain their lifestyles and she gives it to them. Making them indebted to her,"

Bettie and Graham just laughed because it was such a clever idea, and Penelope was clearly using them to kill multiple birds with a single stone.

Bettie hated being used and manipulated like this, she had to stop Penelope's plan from going so well. And judging by Graham's face he was thinking the same.

"We have to solve this quickly. Each hour that passes," Bettie said, "Penelope buys more shares and loses the money of her enemies. If we can solve this quickly then we can support her enemies indirectly and hopefully stop Penelope,"

Graham smiled.

They both had to do that.

They had to stop Penelope's plan.

Bettie just didn't know how stopping it would affect them.

Would Penelope be mad?

Rageful?

Want revenge?

Bettie didn't know.

Not a clue.

CHAPTER 10
8th April 2022
London, England

Graham stood up on the fake-wooden conference table and turned off the air-conditioning unit for Bettie so she couldn't smell any of that foul creamy coffee smell.

Then he simply hopped off the table and kissed her for waiting for him to do it. Graham had always been concerned that Bettie would try to do it herself and risk falling off the table, he was still surprised at how well the baby bump threw off her centre of balance.

"What did Zoey find out?" Bettie asked.

Graham clicked his fingers, sat back down and allowed Bettie to rest her feet on his lap.

He had just come back from visiting Zoey at the Met Police's crime lab (that was even more of a paperwork nightmare. The Met really didn't want Zoey to use *their* labs) and he thankfully had something important to tell Bettie.

The computer virus hadn't erased itself completely.

"There were trace amounts of the computer virus still in the car's systems," Graham said.

Bettie frowned. "How's that possible? I thought Zo said it was completely gone,"

"I don't know. She said that after the car… 'crashed'. It damaged some of the computer systems so the Erase Procedures still didn't manage to get to all of the virus," Graham said.

Bettie smiled and nodded. He agreed it was interesting how computers worked, he just never wanted to study them.

"Did she find anything on the computer virus?" Bettie asked.

"When I left she was finishing up a test of some sort. She should have sent you an email by now,"

Bettie passed over Graham her laptop, and Graham started to check her emails. He wouldn't believe how many baby shops had been selling her things, he had little idea she was so baby obsessed.

"Into baby things after all?" Graham asked, smiling.

She playfully kicked him. "Course. I checked out a few cribs, toys and nursery things,"

Graham blew her a kiss as he started to type in Zoey's email address. The email had to be here somewhere.

"Do you want to get the babies scanned for sex?"

Graham asked, carefully.

Bettie huffed. "I really don't know Gra. But please don't ask me things carefully. You have every right to ask, but I just don't know,"

Graham smiled a little. He only realised now that he wanted a firm yes, he really wanted to know what sex his kid was going to be. He just hoped Bettie would feel the same way at some point.

Then he found the email. He read it.

"Here," Graham said. "Zoey found patented code in the computer virus. It belongs to… CryptoMill Limited,"

Graham was flat shocked at these people. They were careless enough to use their own computer virus to assassinate their own Co-founder.

"Is that enough for a warrant?" Bettie asked.

Graham shook his head. All they had was a massive falling out between two people, a mysterious accident and some computer virus that belonged to the company. A computer virus that Graham wouldn't be surprised to find on the dark web.

They needed more.

"What about the tests of the metal shavings?" Bettie asked.

Graham scanned the very bottom of the email.

"Yep. She tested it and it's your everyday metal alloys. It most probably belongs to a spanner,"

"No chance of giving us a brand?"

Graham shook his head.

Bettie stood up, stretched and walked around the

conference table twice.

"We know someone faked the accident," Bettie said.

"Someone short judging by the mirrors," Graham said, "but have we ever seen the body?"

Bettie smiled and Graham realised that they should have asked the question earlier.

Graham quickly searched for the body on the police databases and frowned.

"The body was cremated two days after the accident. Police thought it was a straightforward crash, no autopsy was done,"

Bettie folded her arms and huffed. Graham wasn't impressed either. That body was properly the only proof they had that something else had happened that night.

"Any photos of the body in the police file?" Bettie asked.

Graham looked at the online version and nodded. There was a single photo of the body from a responding officer, the photo showed the Co-founder's head smashed against the steering wheel with his eyes open.

Graham hated looking at dead people's eyes. They looked so creepy and scary, but there was something off about the eyes. They looked almost cloudy.

Bettie seemed to notice it too. "He officially died in the crash, but no crashes I know produce cloudy eyes,"

"Poisons do," Graham said.

"Where are the ashes being held?" Bettie asked.

Graham looked it up quickly and really hoped they hadn't been scattered already.

He smiled. "They're being held in the Central London Crematorium waiting to be picked up,"

"I think we need Zoey to conduct another test for us," Bettie said.

Graham wasn't sure. It was a long shot but he had heard of police cases where tests were still able to detect poisons if the Crematorium had done a bad job.

He just hoped Central London Crematorium wasn't very good at their job.

THE RUSSIAN CASE

CHAPTER 11
8th April 2022
London, England

Bettie was so excited for the results.

Standing outside the bright sterile white doors of the crime lab in an even brighter white corridor with tens upon tens (it seemed like) labs shooting off from the corridor, Bettie and Graham waited for Zoey to complete her test on the ashes of Finn Ellis and hopefully she could find out something that would explain the cloudiness of his eyes.

Bettie had seen a lot of strange things in her years as a Private Eye but that had to be one of the strangest. No one's eyes should look that cloudy if they had died in a car accident, but with everything going on Bettie already knew for sure the crash had been staged.

Bettie took long shallow breaths as the smell of orange-scented bleach became overwhelming. She didn't know if the smell was actually overwhelming to everyone else, or if her pregnant senses were heightened to help protect her.

But Bettie kept returning to something that had been bugging her for ages ever since she had spoken to Maya of NGD News. Why had Russian Empire News been the only news agency to cover the accident?

Bettie had no delusions about how competitive the different news agencies were, but to think one foreign news agency had managed to fight all the other British agencies away from covering a major UK event. That made absolutely no sense.

"What do you know about Russian Empire News?" Bettie said.

Graham shrugged. "All I know is its broadcasting license is being reviewed by the TV watchdog,"

Bettie frowned a little at that. She thought all Russian channels and news agencies had been sanctioned and banned from the UK after the war broke out, but clearly Russian Empire News had escaped the sanctions.

Bettie took out her phone and ran the name through the various Private Eye databases, and really hoped that it would reveal something.

"My question is how did the news agency manage to keep the Co-Founder accident exclusive," Bettie asked.

Graham nodded. He must have been wondering the same thing, and it was surprising (to Bettie at least) that no security agency had tried to takeover the reporting at all. It was no secret that Russia and China and other dodgy governments were heavily interested in what tech the UK was producing.

So the security agencies were always watching and trying to keep those governments away from stories that might allow them to learn about UK technology.

Bettie just couldn't understand why they didn't on this occasion. Then again Bettie, Sean and Graham all tried to monitor the various technological news sources and yet they hadn't seen anything about CryptoMill besides from when the company tried to hire her.

"Excuse me," a tall man said as he went into the lab.

Bettie knew the tests weren't easy to do but she wished Zoey would hurry up. It had been two hours since Zoey got Graham's phone call, and Bettie and Graham had gone to a wonderful vegan restaurant for a very late lunch.

Bettie clicked her fingers. "You know what I mentioned at lunch about the spanner,"

Graham looked completely blank. Bettie couldn't blame him. They had barely spoken about the case at lunch, Bettie had used it as a chance for them to talk about the future, the baby and their families. For that amazing lunch they really were just another couple in London, and Bettie loved times like that.

"Oh yea," Graham said, "you mentioned the spanner wouldn't be used by anyone from CryptoMill and I laughed,"

Bettie playfully hit him over the head. She didn't like it when he laughed at her but she understood it. It was probably one of the weakest connections she had ever made as a Private Eye, but she still believed it.

"I know a worker at CryptoMill could have bought in a spanner from home. But I doubt it, and the patented software," Bettie said, "and the very short woman changing the mirrors and then there's the Russian Empire News link,"

Graham smiled. "You think we're looking for a professional fixer or an assassin,"

Bettie shook her head at the assassin part. She truly didn't believe someone would hire an assassin to do the job with Finn Ellis, but a fixer would make sense. It would explain everything about the car, the computer virus and the news agency.

Graham jokingly threw his arms up in the air. "Fine then. If there is a professional fixer in the works here, how do we find them?"

"I might be able to help with that," Penelope said as she walked down the corridor towards them like she owned the lab.

Bettie almost laughed at Graham's look of utter horror. She had no idea how Penelope was even allowed in the building given it was attached to a police station, but Bettie had to admire Penelope for her style and sheer ability to own every room she walked into.

"Miss English," Penelope said dipping her head.

"I must say that is a great idea,"

Bettie didn't know whether she should be flattered or not.

"I never would have thought about a fixer Miss English. That was very clever thinking for an English person," Penelope said.

Now Bettie wasn't flattered.

Graham stepped forward. "How did you get in here?"

Penelope gave him a playful smile. "Now, now Detective Adams. Russian money gets you in a lot of places in this playground of a country. Why should a police station be any different?"

Bettie wrapped her arms around Graham's waist to sort of calm him down. He was right though. This was absolutely outrageous and Bettie was somehow going to stop this Russian influence, but that wasn't her focus for now.

Then the bright sterile white lab doors opened. Zoey walked out and shot Penelope a warning look.

Bettie frowned. "You two know each other,"

"Yes," Zoey said, clearly annoyed. "This is the woman who wanted to fund my son's university in a few years' time for a favour,"

Bettie and Graham just stared at Penelope.

"You English people are so... uptight," Penelope said. "I simply wanted to offer Miss Quill some money in exchange for a blood test,"

"Who's?" Bettie asked, coldly.

"That is none of your business. But Miss English,

if you are looking for a fixer. May I gesture you look at Russian Empire News itself? I know from personal experience how easy it is from journalists to surpass government checks at borders,"

Bettie shook her head. Another disgusting detail about Russian infiltration.

"And as your English people stupidly say… good day," Penelope said as she left.

"Hate that woman," Graham said.

"I heard that!" Penelope shouted.

"Good!" Graham shouted.

Bettie laughed and looked back at Zoey. "Results?"

Zoey smiled a little. "Should it be a little too clique to say I found the remains of a finger in the crematorium. They did an awful job and I found traces of a Russian nerve agent,"

Bettie's smile grew. "It would be, but I know you're too good for cliques,"

"Thanks Bet. I managed to trace the nerve agent to a lab in Russia owned by someone living in the UK,"

Graham's mouth dropped. Bettie almost joined him.

"Who?" Bettie asked.

"The Director of Russian Empire News UK. He's currently in London," Zoey said.

Bettie laughed. That was a little too perfect for her liking, but he had to be somehow involved in this case.

Bettie looked at Graham. "Looks like we need to visit some news studios,"

CHAPTER 12
8th April 2022
London, England

After storming the skyscraper with coppers with a search warrant, Graham and Bettie both walked into Russian Empire News UK Director Jaxon Ramsey's office.

Graham didn't like it whatsoever. It was a horribly large office that was probably twenty metres long and another ten metres wide. There was no reason for it to be that big, and considering all the so-called priced Samo-var-things on the walls, Graham didn't like it.

The horrible atmosphere he got from the office was that of a jumped-up little rich boy, and the massive marble desk of Jaxon only confirmed his theory.

But as Graham looked at the desk and saw Jaxon sitting there like he had nothing to worry about with two young police officers keeping him in place, his hate was only growing.

Yet at least Graham finally had a chance to prove to the Russian elite that the UK police force wasn't a joke or toy to be played with. Not that it was in the first place.

Graham looked at Bettie and was thankfully okay even though Graham could smell fresh disgusting pastries near the desk, so hopefully she would just stay away.

"What is the meaning of this," Jaxon said, "I am a citizen and I have my rights. This is an-"

Graham waved him silent. "Mr Ramsey as we speak my officers are searching the entire building. We will be here for hours. Soon people from MI5 will join us. Now as a member of the police force who is nationally recognised for his brilliance I have some pull,"

Graham had no idea if that was true, but he liked to believe it.

"And I can use that pull to help you or destroy you. Russian Empire News is dead. Just accept that,"

"My government will not-" Jaxon started before Bettie shot him a warning look.

"Thanks dear," Graham said smiling. "Your government does not matter here. Your government will not save you. I know that. But lucky for you I am only interested in one particular case,"

Graham almost laughed as he watched Jaxon breathe a massive sigh of relief. He almost wanted to ask how many crimes had he committed for Russia, but Graham knew better than to interfere with MI5's work.

Jaxon slowly stood up. The two police officers looked at Graham. He nodded.

Jaxon walked over to the little cabinet behind the desk and pulled out a rather ornate decanter of something. Probably Russian vodka judging by the colour.

"Stop," Graham said quietly and the police officers grabbed the decanter. "You aren't drinking any poison here,"

Jaxon laughed like that was the most stupidest thing anyone had ever said to him. Maybe it was but Graham was not letting Jaxon die before MI5 got to talk to him.

Graham had far too much respect for them that way.

"I'm interested in the case of Finn Ellis," Graham said.

Bettie came to stand next to Graham. Graham loved the smell of her sweet perfume.

"Mr Ramsey," Bettie pressed.

Jaxon rolled his eyes. "I didn't do it,"

Graham was about to fall in the classic trap of seeing that as a denial, but Jaxon wasn't denying it completely.

"I know you didn't do it. But a nerve agent from a factory you own did," Graham said.

Jaxon's eyebrows rosed at that, and Graham was a little bit surprised. He almost seemed as if he had no idea about that particular nerve agent.

"What do you know?" Graham asked.

Jaxon looked at the two police officers that were trapping him here. "Does he actually have power?"

Both officers nodded. They really nodded as if that was actually true. Graham started to feel good about himself.

"Fine then," Jaxon said. "The plan was simple enough. I was just to follow some instructions about reporting what was said,"

Bettie folded her arms. "So the accident didn't happen?"

"Course not," Jaxon said, "I was given a pack of information and told to report it. It's how the Russian state promotes its propaganda in the Motherland,"

Graham and Bettie rolled their eyes. Graham hated that about dictators.

"Who gave you the information package?" Bettie asked.

There was a knock on the door and another police officer and two men in black suits walked in.

Graham recognised the police officer as someone belonging to the Met police who was helping him search the building. The two men in suits were clearly MI5. That was only confirmed when they showed him their IDs.

"Detective Adams," the taller man said, "I have been ordered to transport this man away immediately,"

The shorter of the two men went over to Jaxon.

Graham nodded. "Just one question please,"

The taller man nodded.

"Answer her question," Graham said pointing to Bettie.

Jaxon gestured that he needed to hear the question again.

"Who gave you the information package?" she asked.

Jaxon smiled. "The Protectorate of Russian London,"

Jaxon smashed his face on the desk.

The MI5 men rushed over.

But it was too late. Jaxon's mouth was all foamy and his eyes were completely cloudy.

Graham and Bettie just looked at each other.

They had a name.

But it was a name he didn't know.

It sounded like the name of a terrorist.

And that absolutely terrified Graham.

CHAPTER 13
9th April 2022
London, England

Bettie held her nose as she went into the conference room in the police station with the fake-wooden conference table and glass walls around her, she hated the smell of the cops' coffee in the morning.

She was so jealous of them!

Graham walked in behind her carrying a glass of lemon tea for her, and some disgusting green tea for him. Bettie was not a fan of green tea in the slightest, it was so bitter and it left such a strange taste in her mouth. She much preferred the lemony sweetness of her tea.

Bettie put her laptop on the table and fired it up. She had to find out what the crime scene techs discovered after last night's excitement where Jaxon Ramsey had caused a fake tooth to break and release a nerve agent into his body.

It was a coward's way to go out!

Thankfully she had managed to get to sleep in a hotel even with Graham's constant tossing and turning in the night. He was clearly concerned about the so-called Ghost of Russian London.

But Bettie couldn't find anything about it.

"Morning," an elderly man said as he walked in with a massive mug filled with a hazelnut latte.

Bettie just looked at Graham and he thankfully took the mug outside. Leaving the elderly man looking rather confused about the situation.

Then Bettie realised that the man was wearing a tight black suit and his hair was perfectly combed, tailored and expertly cut. This man clearly had money so she was guessing he was the police captain of the station.

"Sorry about that Tre," Graham said, "Bet's a bit sensitive to animal products. You know hormones, pregnancy and everything,"

Bettie wanted to hit this Trevor as he rolled his eyes like this was just so typical of women.

"It's okay," Trevor said. "I hear you wanted to know about the Ghost of Russian London?"

Bettie nodded. It made sense the police captain would know of any major criminals in the local area.

"The Ghost of Russian London, or Ghost R as we prefer to call them is a ghost. No one has ever seen, heard or even confirmed they existed," Trevor said.

Bettie searched her Private Eye databases for any

mention of the person.

"How did you first hear about them?" Bettie asked.

Trevor rubbed his forehead. "There was a bombing about three decades ago. Witnesses reported seeing a woman dressed in white as she launched a bomb that made the sky burn orange and rain down death upon the enemy of the Motherland,"

Bettie and Graham just looked at each other. That was a bit of a strange witness statement.

"I should probably add that witness was an English Literature Student," Trevor said.

Bettie nodded. That explained it.

"Then," Trevor said. "Ghost R has been believed to be behind explosions, deaths and crimes all over the world. A bombing in the USA in 2000. A kidnapping in France in 2014. The assassination of a Foreign Minster in Sydney in 2015,"

Graham frowned. "Then why are they called the Ghost of Russian London?"

Trevor nodded thoughtfully. Bettie hated it when people did that.

"Because their crimes started here. The crimes are done with such a flare that it's easy to see the crimes are committed by the same person,"

Bettie's laptop beeped as the scan through the databases was complete and there was not a single mention of the Ghost of Russian London. She didn't know if that was concerning or not, considering some of those databases were government ones.

Graham was about to open his mouth, but Bettie waved him silent. She wanted to try something a bit more direct considering they didn't have long left to stop CryptoMill from invalidating the western sanctions.

"We know the Ghost R has to be a fixer for local Russians," Bettie said smiling, "so we need to someone to hire them for us,"

"We cannot hire Penelope," Trevor and Graham said.

Bettie shrugged. "We…"

Bettie wanted to protest her case but something wasn't adding up. Ghost R was simply a middle man (or woman) who always worked for someone to fix their problems.

That was who they were actually after, so ideally they need to find the person who hired Ghost R, and not the fixer itself. And Bettie knew the second they actually found Ghost R every single intelligence service from London to Washington to Sydney would probably be after such a legendary fixer.

That would waste too much time.

Bettie was going to have to find the hirer of Ghost R a different way. Maybe even a little impersonation.

"How would someone hire Ghost R?" Bettie asked.

Trevor shook his head. "Miss English, I am not-"

"I don't want to hire them myself. I want to be a lot more direct. I want to impersonate them when I talk to Jade Fox,"

Graham smiled. "Babe, I love you and all. But you have a problem,"

"What?" Bettie asked.

Graham and Trevor just pointed to the baby bump.

"Babe, I doubt Ghost R is going to be pregnant,"

Bettie smiled and nodded. She had slightly forgotten about that.

And each of them knew for a fact that Ghost R would have been hired anomalously so no one would actually know what they looked like or even their sex. The cover was quite perfect, and that only got Bettie even more excited.

"Miss English, Graham could probably pull it off. And you're a Private Eye after all. You could pretend to have a Russian Accent," Trevor said.

Bettie coughed a little and spoke in a near-perfect accent.

"What accent? This is how I always talk Comrade,"

Graham laughed. "Bettie, Comrade's a bit much,"

Bettie laughed. This was going to be great fun.

Pretending to be Russian assassins for hire.

Bettie couldn't think of a better way to spend a morning.

Bettie only had one chance.

But what happened if the real Ghost R found out?

And what if the real Ghost R didn't like it?

CHAPTER 14
9th April 2022
London, England

This was outrageous.

Graham could hardly say he was impressed pretending to be a disgusting Russian assassin so he could get the truth out of Jade Fox.

A short slim man in a tight business suit led Graham and Bettie into a massively posh conference room with floor-to-ceiling windows that allowed Graham to see all of London (that was hundreds of metres below him), a solid marble conference table and rather alarmingly there were tons of Russian things lining the outside of the room.

Graham hated to see how many Russian tea tins, cups and so many of those damn samovar-things that Graham still hated with a passion.

This was one of the most disgusting places he had ever been to. Even the so-called Russian tea that Graham could smell was an insult on London and the pure righteousness of English breakfast tea.

Wow. Graham was starting to realise how much he really didn't like Russians during this case.

"Detective Adams, Miss English," Jade Fox said as she walked into the conference room and sat and the head of the table.

Graham and Bettie sat on the table and frowned at her.

It was show time.

Whilst Graham and Bettie had on their normal clothes, Graham was not a fan of Jade's pink flowery dress that was too tight for her in several places. At least she looked nice and innocent for her role in all this he supposed.

"Where's our money?" Graham said in a perfect Russian accent.

Jade only smiled. "I'm sorry,"

Bettie kicked Jade in the leg. "You said you'll pay us by now,"

Graham was impressed. Her accent made her sound like she had always been Russian.

Jade's smile deepened. "I'm really sorry. I don't have time for this. I do not know what you are talking about,"

Graham grabbed her wrist. "Do you want us to explain to your workers how you paid out to kill your Co-Founder and create a misinformation package for Russian Empire News?"

"Shit," Jade said.

Then she sat back down and put her face in her

hands.

"You didn't pay us," Bettie said again.

"I..." Jade said.

"What?" Graham asked. "You think because we were invisible we wouldn't want to get paid,"

Jade nodded then stood up and cocked her head.

"Wait! You two can't be the Ghost. I read in the police report the car mirrors were changed for a short person to drive the car. I doubt Miss English was driving,"

Bettie looked offended and outraged. Graham loved her commitment to acting.

"How dare you!" Bettie shouted. "Do you know how many stupid English people I deceive with this fake bump?"

Graham almost laughed at that. She was clever.

"This is why I kill you pathetic English people. You are all so weak, jumped up and outrageous. You are so easy to fool," Bettie said.

Jade frowned and sat back down, but at least Graham now knew that the Ghost of Russian London was behind the mirrors changing, the smashing of the lights and information package to the RE news.

There was only one question that bothered him.

Graham placed his hands firmly on Jade's shoulders.

"You also broke our agreement about hiring another fixer," Graham said, lying. "You said you wouldn't hire anyone, but the police knew everything about the setup,"

Bettie kicked Jade in the leg.

Jade started crying. "I only did this for the Motherland. I did really. I just wanted to help your people,"

Graham just shook his head. "We need a name!"

Jade cried more and more. "I don't know! A man called me knowing everything. He said he would handle the police. Please! Don't kill me,"

Graham just looked at Bettie and smiled. Bettie nodded back. They both knew that was all they were going to get from Jade Fox. Sure she might be intentionally trying to help the Russian people because maybe they didn't deserve to suffer for their president's criminal actions.

But Graham just wasn't sure she was a bad guy. It was clear she was uninformed about the Russians and she clearly didn't understand how her allowing money to enter Russia would invalidate all western sanctions and only empower Russia to invade more countries.

Yet Graham still wasn't sure she was a bad person.

Graham and Bettie started laughing.

Jade stood up looking furious. "You two lied to me! I thought I was going to die!"

Jade looked at Bettie and her hands formed fists.

Graham stood up. His hands formed fists. His eyes narrowed on jade.

How dare she look at Bettie like that.

"Listen here you!" Graham shouted. "You will not expand into Russia. Your stupid ideals could cause World War Three. You will stop now,"

Jade laughed. "You are all the same. The Russian people don't deserve to suffer. We would be targeting the president and his friends, not the economy that targets the innocent people,"

Graham just huffed. This woman clearly didn't understand what the West was doing and targeting the economy was another measurement against the president and his friends. Graham just didn't have time for uninformed people anymore.

Graham got out the handcuffs. "Jade Fox I am arresting you for murder,"

As Graham read Jade her rights and escorted her out of the building, he was more than glad he was finally stopping her stupid ambitions that threatened everyone he loved.

But there was something else that was troubling him.

Who claimed to know everything about the Co-Founder's death and who alerted the police?

CHAPTER 15
9th April 2022
London, England

Bettie sat at the opposite end of the fake-wooden conference table as she searched some databases on her laptop whilst Graham sat at the other end tasting a disgusting and rather foul smelling beefburger.

"Who would have access to Jade, Ghost R and the police?" Graham asked with a full mouth of burger.

Bettie frowned as her databases revealed nothing about any Russian influence in any Met police forces, not even the station they were in.

"I don't know," Bettie said. "But I think we need to focus on what Jade said. And by the way, what happened to her?"

Graham gave her a dirty smile. He clearly enjoyed arresting Jade.

"I handed her over to MI5. They wanted to see if she was working for any Russians or knew their plans,"

"Do you think she does?" Bettie asked.

Graham shrugged. "It's possible. I doubted Jade knew how to expand into Russia and get enough money to go on the London Stock exchange by herself,"

Bettie clicked her fingers and Graham finished up his burger and smiled. That was the key to all of this.

"You mentioned to me last night," Bettie said, "you were surprised that CryptoMill had enough money to make it on the Exchange,"

Graham nodded.

"What if you were right and they had help?" Bettie asked.

Graham finished licking his fingers. Bettie hated it when he did that. It was gross.

"It would make sense," Graham said. "Oo and I spoke to the MI5 guy who took her from me. Turns out CryptoMill knew how to bend the law in such a way that it wasn't illegal,"

Bettie just shook her head. That was strange and she couldn't even begin to imagine the legal complexities of doing such a thing.

"Who the hell could have managed that legal argument?" Bettie asked.

"Not a local law firm that's for sure," Graham said with a smile.

Bettie went back to her laptop. They were clearly looking for someone who had a lot of money, knew law or knew people who knew law and had influence, because there was still the police connection.

Bettie looked up the most powerful and wealthiest Russian men still in London, and conducted a quick background check on them. There were thankfully only five names.

"Jade told us," Graham said, getting out his phone, "that a man called her,"

"And?" Bettie said, not focusing on him.

Bettie heard Graham tapping away at his phone and then he laughed.

"What?" Bettie asked as the background checks were almost complete.

"The only odd phone call Jade got in the three days after the murder was from a blocked number in the East end of London,"

Bettie smiled and spun around her laptop. Graham gestured her to come closer but she wasn't sure if he smelt of horrible beef burger.

She risked it.

Bettie carefully walked down to the other end of the fake-wooden table and showed Graham one of the names she had run. Thankfully he didn't stink of beefburger.

"Who's this? Name's a bit English?" Graham said.

Bettie shook her head. "This is a Russian Oligarch he changed his name to Grayson Yarbury in 2008. He came to the UK, set up a profitable business and in 2016 he got friendly with the government and he was made a Lord,"

Bettie could only smile as she watched the rage, anger and frustration build in Graham's face. It was quite the show, but she understood his annoyance. It was flat out wrong that all these rich, posh people needed to do was offer the government some money and they were allowed in the House of Lords.

A position that gave a person direct power over UK politics.

"And this Lord lives in the East End of London and he always uses a blocked number,"

Graham didn't look pleased. "This isn't enough Bet. If we're going to investigate a Lord we need a lot more evidence than he lived in the same place,"

Bettie tapped her laptop and checked who owned stock in CryptoMill. He didn't own any so there was no way to prove he even knew about CrytoMill that way.

"We could call him?" Bettie asked with a grin.

Graham cocked his head and looked like he was going to say no. "Pass me your laptop,"

Bettie did it. "Why?"

Graham started typing away at it. "Because I want to login into my police accounts. There's a new piece of software that allows us to compare voices on phones and in videos,"

"So you want to see if the person who answers the call if the same person? Bit of a long shot," Bettie said.

Graham pulled up the software and just looked at

her.

"Babe. Do you have a better idea?"

Bettie didn't. This was probably their last chance to see who phoned Jade that night, and this Lord Grayson was the only person with a background check that seemed a little strange.

There was no one else who it could be.

Bettie watched Graham plug in a video of Lord Grayson speaking in the House of Lords and then he connected Bettie's phone to the laptop.

"Go for it," Graham said.

Bettie dialled the phone number that rang Jade that night.

It dialled for three rings.

Someone picked up.

"Hello," a man said in a posh English voice.

"Hello," Bettie said, "I am legal counsellor for Jade Fox and I was wondering if I could ask you a few questions,"

"I am don't know you Miss. I do not know a Jade Fox. I bid you a good day," the man said cutting the line.

Bettie looked at the computer software. The voice in the video and on the phone didn't match.

Then Bettie watched the video of Lord Grayson sitting down and another Lord standing up and started talking.

The computer software flashed. The two voices matched.

Bettie laughed. They needed to find out who that

other Lord was.
    Urgently.

CHAPTER 16
9th April 2022
London, England

Graham was seriously getting annoyed now. Did this government and Russian corruption never end?

Graham and Bettie stood at one end of the fake-wooden conference table and at the other was a horrible elderly man in a tight tailored black suit from MI5 and a wonderful and very tall woman dressed in a black dress. She was the head of the Met police.

Graham was a bit surprised at how young she was, but at this point he just cared for an ally.

"We cannot interview him," the MI5 man said.

Graham was getting so tired of hearing that. it was disgraceful that just because someone was a Lord it meant so many people were scared of talking to them.

That was why Graham had pushed so hard to allow Bettie (a civilian in the eyes of others) access to the case. He needed someone outside of the police bureaucracy.

Graham still hated everything about Lord Nathan Blake. He sounded like a perfectly good man, he loved his country, loved his family and he was actually making sure what he did in the world made a positive difference.

Something Graham could say about so few people these days in politics.

But Graham couldn't interview him under a police caution that would apparently be too dangerous for all of their careers.

"We have to interview him," Graham said.

"Your software proved that Lord Nathan Blake is the same man who phoned Jade in the three days after the murder. He knew about the crime. He did nothing," Bettie said.

Graham couldn't disagree with that. Even if his Lordship was innocent that alone was strange.

"Miss English this is of no business of yours," the MI5 man said.

"What's your name for crying out loud?" Bettie asked.

"I'm Intelligence Officer Daniels. That's all you need to know,"

Graham didn't like the name. They wouldn't be calling their kids that.

"Good," Bettie said, "but I think my good personal friend Skylar Mason the Justice secretary would like me on this case,"

That shut up Daniels. Graham had forgotten

their friend in the heart of the government who would always help them after solving a case for her last week.

"This never ends!" Daniels shouted.

Bettie stepped forward. "What doesn't?"

Daniels frowned. "All these politicians. We need answers and action right now. You have a government that doesn't want to sanction Russians and are purposefully going too slow. Then you have all the government's Russian friends in the House of Lords,"

Graham was starting to understand the state and pressure MI5 must be under because how the hell do you keep the UK safe when a few of the bad guys are in the heart of politics?

An area the security services cannot investigate unless the government says they can.

That reminded Graham. "So *you* can't interview the Lord?"

Daniels threw his arms up in the air. "No. Not unless someone in government tells us to, or that we're allowed,"

Graham and Bettie just smiled at each other.

Graham pulled Bettie close. "Well Miss English, I think you need to make a phone call to the Justice Secretary,"

"I think so too Mr Adams," Bettie said, grinning.

And Graham was surprised to see Daniels and the Met Police Chief actually smiling. He didn't think those two could do that.

Bettie made the phone call.

CHAPTER 17
9th April 2022
London, England

Bettie was so excited about learning the truth.

"Why did you call Jade Fox?" Graham asked Lord Nathan Blake.

Bettie had been expecting the Lord to be taller, larger and stronger than anyone else in the conference room as everyone sat around the large fake-wooden conference table with her, Graham and Officer Daniels at one end and his so-called Lordship down at the other.

But it turned out Nathan Blake was just a normal posh jumped-up man with his silk tailored suit and posh expensive watches and walking stick. It was clear to Bettie that he didn't need a walking stick, but she supposed it was more than status rather than anything else.

Bettie still wasn't a fan of his wooden, piney aftershave that was starting to stink out the conference room.

"I didn't call Jade Fox that night," Nathan said.

Bettie just folded her arms and clearly Daniels wasn't impressed either.

"We have matched your voice to from a phone call with Jade on the night of a murder. You clearly know something,"

"The Murder?" Nathan asked. "Young man I do not know of any such murder. I am an English Lord and I know what that means. I uphold the English laws,"

Bettie really hoped he didn't break down into some strange nationalist speech. She would probably have to hit him, or simply breathe in too much of his aftershave, smell the animal product and vomit all over him.

That was a lot more her style.

"Where were you on the night the phone call was made?" Graham asked, passing the Lord the phone records.

Bettie wasn't too hopeful.

"Oh yes kind sir," Nathan said. "I know exactly where I was. It was a jolly good show too,"

"You went to the theatre?" Bettie asked.

"Oh no. I was… I am not going to answer that question,"

Daniels shook his head. "My Lord, this is a matter of national security and if you do love this country as much as you say you do. Then you will answer these questions or I'll find out and I will personally leak it to the press,"

"Oh no. don't. Please don't," Daniels said.

Bettie always loved it when other people did the dirty work for her. She was fully intending to report all the dodgy people in this investigation to Maya of NGD News anyway. Just because they were rich and powerful didn't mean their crimes didn't deserve to be shared.

"I was with a young girl," Nathan said slowly.

"A call girl?" Daniels said.

"Good god man," Nathan said. "I wouldn't go and do such a disgraceful thing,"

Bettie just smiled. Only a Lord would have such an over-the-top reaction to a simple question.

"I was with a young girl I know. She just turned twenty so I was… showing her the ropes,"

Bettie just wanted to be sick. She would never want to "do the act" with such an old man at her age.

"Where was this?" Graham asked.

"In my cottage from the motorway on that cold lonely night,"

Bettie slammed her fists on the table as she feared Nathan might start to reveal some details.

Nathan looked at her in shock. "No one has ever slammed their fists at me before. That is outrageous. You clearly aren't English,"

Wow! Bettie was definitely going to give his name to Maya.

Graham stood up. "Wait your cottage. So you saw what happened?"

"That makes no sense," Bettie said. "Why would a Lord have a cottage next to a motorway?"

"Unless," Daniels said, "he wasn't staying at his cottage. He was staying at hers,"

Nathan frowned. "Fine I was staying with a young girl called Eva Pierce,"

"Bastard," Daniels said.

Bettie and Graham just looked at each other. There was clearly something to that name, something criminal.

"There's nothing wrong with her. She's a wonderful girl. Very flexible,"

Bettie waved Nathan silent.

Daniels gestured Bettie and Graham to come over to him and he started whispering.

"Eva Pierce is a former UK citizen turned Russian asset," Daniels said. "She works for the Kremlin directly and I believe she has been behind three assassinations in the past year on high-level government targets,"

"What does that mean?" Bettie asked.

Daniels shrugged.

Bettie just looked at Nathan again and he was smiling. She didn't understand why he would be smiling of all people, he was locked in a conference room with a Private Eye, a cop and a person from MI5.

There was nothing to be happy about.

Bettie looked through the glass walls to see if any known criminals were about and she didn't see any.

Bettie didn't even see Penelope.

There was no reason for him to be smiling.

Unless there was no Eva Pierce and Nathan hadn't been with a girl in the first place.

Bettie frowned. "You're lying to us,"

Nathan looked offended. "I am not,"

"Eva Pierce was killed a week ago in Paris," Bettie said, lying coldly.

Nathan opened his mouth. He started stuttering. He couldn't get the words out.

Bettie knew he was lying. He must have read about Eva Pierce in some security briefing and learnt of her that way. She must have been the perfect tempting carrot for Nathan to drop in front of anyone who got too close to his truth.

Bettie went round to the other side of the fake-wooden conference table and opened up her laptop. She quickly searched to see how much Stock he had in CryptoMill.

None.

Then Bettie reran the search to see how much had he had in the company before Jade got arrested.

Over two million pounds worth and the extremely odd thing about all this was he had that many shares before the company even went on the Stock Exchange.

He was the man who gave Jade the money.

Bettie smiled and tutted. "Tell me Nathan, given the stock price for CryptoMill is £1. How much money did you lose?"

Nathan shook his head and laughed. "There's no point denying it now is there?"

Graham and Daniels slowly nodded as they finally caught up with everything.

"No," Graham said. "You were the man who gave Jade Fox the money to buy their way onto the Stock Exchange,"

"You knew Jade's ambitions for Russia," Bettie said. "You also knew the Co-Founder was a risk to that plan. So what? You told her to get rid of him?"

Nathan simply pulled out his chair and put his feet up on the table like he was in complete control of the situation. Bettie hated people like him.

"It was simple really. She jumped at the idea. Then I only introduced her to the Ghost of Russian London and that was that," Nathan said.

"Jade ordered the killing of the Co-Founder. The Ghost did it and laid all the breadcrumbs and you cashed in on the Stock Exchange," Bettie said.

Nathan simply nodded.

After all the complexities and weirdness of this case, Bettie had wondered if the case was going to come back to some crazy Russian plot with massive political ramifications and whilst the case did have some of them.

This all came back to money.

It all came back to some jumped-up Lord wanting to make a boatload of money regardless of if it risked the security of the entire world and might even cause World War Three.

Bettie shook her head at Nathan. "Jade lied, didn't she? You didn't call her that night to tell her you knew? And that you would sort out the police so they would believe it was a speeding crash?"

Nathan smiled. "Miss English. I… called her to make sure she was okay and she knew that everything had been taken care of,"

Graham stepped forward. "The Policing angle though…"

Bettie and Graham both spun around as they saw Daniels laughing. He was the reason Nathan looked so in control of the situation.

"How better than to make sure the police believed something than making an MI5 officer handle that part? What you do Daniels?" Graham asked. "Hack the police systems, plant evidence and make sure the car got into evidence without examination,"

Daniel nodded. "But it isn't what you think?"

Nathan's face went white.

Daniels took out his handcuffs and walked over to Nathan. "Lord Nathan Blake I am arresting you for treason, espionage and I am probably make up a few more charges for you,"

Bettie waved Daniels to slow down. "You were investigating him,"

"Yep, but I needed you two to help me figure it all out. Me, MI5 and Her Majesty thanks you both,"

As Bettie and Graham watched Daniels escort Nathan away, she was a bit concerned that this was another con or deception. But when she saw another five men and women dressed in black suits walk out of the lift. Bettie knew that wasn't the case.

For some reason MI5 was taking Nathan Blake very seriously, but as far as Bettie was concerned that was far, far, far above her paygrade.

As far as she was concerned, her case was over.

But there was still one more thing she wanted to wrap up.

She needed to see Penelope a final time.

CHAPTER 18
9th April 2022
Canterbury, England

After a meeting with Skylar Mason, the (idiot) Prime Minister and the Head of MI5, Graham was so glad to be back in Canterbury and walking along the amazing high street.

Graham loved the warm feeling of the cobblestoned street under his feet, the cool evening air that wasn't too hot and wasn't too cold. It was just right. And Graham loved the talking, laughing and chatting of the university students as they simply went on with their evening.

Most of them were probably going to clubs, parties or whatever else university students did these days. But just seeing them happy, safe and alright made Graham feel so much better after the past few days.

Even with the amazing little shops that lined the high street open, earning money and simply being able to make a living for themselves made Graham smile. He wasn't sure why but it was probably because it showed that the world was normal to him.

After the past few days Graham had to admit the world was crazy, messed up and awful place at times. But it was wonderful scenes like the high street that made it all better to Graham.

In the meeting he just returned from the MI5 had offered him a part time job but Graham didn't even consider it. As much as he loved all four nations of the UK he didn't want to leave Canterbury or Kent. This was his home and there was certainly more than enough crime to keep him busy here.

And to be honest, Graham didn't want to have to deal with all the politics of London. There was definitely too much red tape for him, but London in small doses would be great.

Graham just shook his head at that idea. It was only a few days ago he was saying that he hated London, but maybe it wasn't so bad after all.

London wasn't a bad place per se, and Graham knew that everything would only get better in time, and Graham knew that Skylar Mason wouldn't let the government repeat the same mistakes over and over and over again.

Changes would be made. Heads would roll. The UK would be safer.

And Graham truly believed that. If Graham, a lone cop from Kent, and his sexy Private Eye girlfriend could make a massive difference in the world. Then Graham was sure that the world would change because of this case and in the bitter end the Russian war would stop.

That's what this was truly about to Graham. Sure he wanted to protect the UK, national security and that stuff. But Graham was only a cop because he wanted to protect innocent people, as he was never going to fly over to the war and fight for those innocent people.

But that didn't mean he couldn't help them in some small way.

Some people might stupidly say that what he did today was meaningless, Russia would find another way or be given another way to invalidate the sanctions. But that was the point.

Graham had stopped the Cryptocurrency sector from being that way for the Russians. Graham knew from his years of experience that other companies watched their competitors and with NGD News making the fall of CrytoMill so public. Graham knew that no other Cryptocurrency firm in the UK or aboard would dare to help the Russians.

So the world was definitely safer on that front.

Graham continued to walk down the amazing high street with the wonderful hints of coffee, alcohol and pastries filling the air from nearby cafes and bars, until he stopped outside the staircase that led up to Bettie's office.

Now that the case was firmly put to bed and everything else was tomorrow's problem, Graham was filled with excitement at seeing his amazing sexy girlfriend not as a partner, but as his lover for the first time in a good few days.

He was looking forward to that.

A lot.

CHAPTER 19
9th April 2022
Canterbury, England

"Thank you Maya,"

As Bettie put the phone down after finishing sending Maya of NGD News all the different pieces of information on the case so she could publicly broadcast it, Bettie was more than grateful to be back in her office.

Bettie loved the feeling of her amazing desk chair, her large wooden desk and the warmth of her office. It was flat out great to be back after the past few chaotic days.

With Graham having his "private" meeting with the government and other officials, Bettie had been so grateful that her nephew Sean had driven up to London to get her (turns out the train drivers were striking). Then Bettie had booked an appointment that Graham would love and then Bettie and Sean had had a wonderful spot of dinner at a nearby café before she returned to her office.

Bettie could still taste the warming succulent vegan chicken on her tongue with its crispy skin and wonderful aromas that still made her mouth water. She would definitely be going back there.

And as much as Bettie could have taken another mode of transport home. Bettie just wanted to see a young person, a young person filled with life and all the childish innocence that came with that.

Sean might have been at university, over 20 and in a very active relationship, but to Bettie he was still her little nephew, and it was people like him that she did what she did for.

She had heard Graham's reasons, before and Bettie completely agreed with him. Bettie always wanted to keep the innocent people safe, secure and protected from the horrors of the world.

But there was another reason why she worked on this case in particular, to Bettie this was more of a preventive measurement just case. Just in case the Russians did decide to get a little more ambitious and in the end they did attack the UK.

Bettie didn't even want to think about that with her own child on the way, but if the Russians did somehow take the UK. Then she didn't want anyone getting hurt, but especially Sean.

The Russians would probably kill Sean straight away for being gay, and Bettie was never going to let that happen.

So if anyone ever asked her why she did what she

did today, that would be her answer. To protect the people she loved whether they were gay or not.

The wonderful sounds of people talking, laughing and even a bit of pop music was playing in the high street below made Bettie smile and it only confirmed her point. She loved all those people.

The wooden door opened and Bettie went to get up thinking it was Graham, but Penelope walked in wearing a long white summer dress and took a seat in front of Bettie.

Bettie could only clap her hands. "You're a clever person I'll give you that,"

Penelope pretended to take a bow. "Now, now Miss English. I only made my enemies lose their money, my assets are safe from the UK government and now I have a lot of power in Glorious Moscow,"

"How much did you lose?" Bettie asked.

"None of my money of course. In fact Miss English I'm up a hundred thousand of your pounds. But my enemies lost four hundred million between them,"

Bettie coughed at that amount. No wonder these Oligarchs were being targeted so much, they had far too much money put together.

"And before you asked Miss English," Penelope said, "I am already using all the favours these people own me to my advantage,"

Bettie leant back in her chair and folded her arms.

"How?"

Penelope gave her a devilish grin. "We both know what this case was truly about,"

Bettie nodded. "You were using us to take out your enemies and get you more power,"

Penelope bowed again. "Of course. And your government will find out soon enough so you might as well be the first to know,"

Bettie felt her stomach twist.

"It turns out the Glorious President no longer trusts the Foreign Minister. So she appointed me as the New Foreign Minister,"

Bettie had no idea if that was good or not. Then Bettie wondered about how far did Penelope's ambitions go.

"Will you seek to become…" Bettie said.

She was about to ask if Penelope wanted to become the Russian President but she knew that was a stupid question. Of course she did.

Penelope stood up. "I must go Miss English. A plane to Moscow leaves shortly. But ask yourself this, would me as a president be so bad?"

Bettie honestly didn't know. Penelope seemed to at least have a respect for democracy, freedom and freedom of speech. But even Bettie couldn't tell if it was all a scheme and façade she put on, but if Penelope truly believed it.

"You can't be much worse than the current one," Bettie said, coldly.

Penelope smiled like that was a funny joke.

Penelope looked like she was about to leave

when Bettie waved her hands at her.

"The blood test?" Bettie asked.

Penelope's evil grin only grew. "Now, now Miss English. We all have our secrets. There is a lot you can test for in blood. Illnesses, DNA and even poisons,"

Bettie wasn't going to let her go that easily.

"You were looking at illnesses, weren't you?" Bettie said.

It was the only thing that fitted with Penelope's power hungry mindset.

Penelope nodded. "Miss English, if an illness is already present in the blood. Then medical examiners don't care if they find it again in the future,"

Bettie was about to ask another question but Penelope just gave her a childish smile. Bettie took that as a sign to be quiet for some reason.

"Until we met again Miss English. And believe me. We will," Penelope said leaving the office.

As much as Bettie didn't like Penelope for her deception, ambitions and being so close to the Russian government, she had to admit Penelope had style.

"What was Penelope doing here?" Graham asked as he came through the door.

Bettie felt her stomach flip with butterflies as she had been really looking forward to seeing him. Not as a partner but as a very hot boyfriend.

Bettie stood up with her laptop and wrapped her free arm around Graham's fit waist and started to lead him out of the office.

"I only just got here," Graham said.

"Well my love," Bettie said, grinning. "We have half an hour to get to the maternity unit at the Hospital. We're going to find out the sexes of our baby,"

Bettie loved seeing Graham's eyes fill with tears and her own eyes did the same, and he kissed her again and again. She knew that before now neither one of them had known how badly they wanted to know.

They had simply been far too scared to know.

But that changed now.

As Bettie and Graham went out of the office, Bettie was so looking forward to finally knowing and whatever happened next they would sort it out together, and it would be the start of the next beautiful chapter in their lives.

And Bettie couldn't wait for that.

GET YOUR FREE AND EXCLUSIVE SHORT STORY NOW! LEARN ABOUT NEMESIO'S PAST!

https://www.subscribepage.com/fireheart

Keep up to date with exclusive deals on Connor Whiteley's Books, as well as the latest news about new releases and so much more!

Sign up for the Grab a Book and Chill Monthly newsletter, and you'll get one **FREE** ebook just for signing up: Agents of The Emperor Collection.

Sign Up Now!

https://dl.bookfunnel.com/f4p5xkprbk

About the author:

Connor Whiteley is the author of over 60 books in the sci-fi fantasy, nonfiction psychology and books for writer's genre and he is a Human Branding Speaker and Consultant.

He is a passionate Warhammer 40,000 reader, psychology student and author.

Who narrates his own audiobooks and he hosts The Psychology World Podcast.

All whilst studying Psychology at the University of Kent, England.

Also, he was a former Explorer Scout where he gave a speech to the Maltese President in August 2018 and he attended Prince Charles' 70th Birthday Party at Buckingham Palace in May 2018.

Plus, he is a self-confessed coffee lover!

Other books by Connor Whiteley:

Bettie English Private Eye Series
A Very Private Woman
The Russian Case
A Very Urgent Matter
A Case Most Personal
Trains, Scots and Private Eyes
The Federation Protects

The Fireheart Fantasy Series
Heart of Fire
Heart of Lies
Heart of Prophecy
Heart of Bones
Heart of Fate

City of Assassins (Urban Fantasy)
City of Death
City of Martyrs
City of Pleasure
City of Power

Agents of The Emperor
Return of The Ancient Ones
Vigilance
Angels of Fire
Kingmaker

The Garro Series- Fantasy/Sci-fi
GARRO: GALAXY'S END
GARRO: RISE OF THE ORDER
GARRO: END TIMES
GARRO: SHORT STORIES
GARRO: COLLECTION
GARRO: HERESY
GARRO: FAITHLESS
GARRO: DESTROYER OF WORLDS
GARRO: COLLECTIONS BOOK 4-6
GARRO: MISTRESS OF BLOOD
GARRO: BEACON OF HOPE
GARRO: END OF DAYS

Winter Series- Fantasy Trilogy Books
WINTER'S COMING
WINTER'S HUNT
WINTER'S REVENGE
WINTER'S DISSENSION

Miscellaneous:
RETURN
FREEDOM
SALVATION
Reflection of Mount Flame
The Masked One
The Great Deer

OTHER SHORT STORIES BY CONNOR WHITELEY

Blade of The Emperor

Arbiter's Truth

The Bloodied Rose

Asmodia's Wrath

Heart of A Killer

Emissary of Blood

Computation of Battle

Old One's Wrath

Puppets and Masters

Ship of Plague

Interrogation

Edge of Failure

One Way Choice

Acceptable Losses

Balance of Power

Good Idea At The Time

Escape Plan

Escape In The Hesitation

Inspiration In Need

Singing Warriors

Dragon Coins

Dragon Tea

Dragon Rider

Knowledge is Power

Killer of Polluters

Climate of Death

Sacrifice of the Soul

Heart of The Flesheater

Heart of The Regent
Heart of The Standing
Feline of The Lost
Heart of The Story
The Family Mailing Affair
Defining Criminality
The Martian Affair
A Cheating Affair
The Little Café Affair
Mountain of Death
Prisoner's Fight
Claws of Death
Bitter Air
Honey Hunt
Blade On A Train
City of Fire
Awaiting Death
Poison In The Candy Cane
Christmas Innocence
You Better Watch Out
Christmas Theft
Trouble In Christmas
Smell of The Lake
Problem In A Car
Theft, Past and Team
Embezzler In The Room
A Strange Way To Go
A Horrible Way To Go
Ann Awful Way To Go
An Old Way To Go

A Fishy Way To Go
A Pointy Way To Go
A High Way To Go
A Fiery Way To Go
A Glassy Way To Go
A Chocolatey Way To Go
Kendra Detective Mystery Collection Volume 1
Kendra Detective Mystery Collection Volume 2
Stealing A Chance At Freedom
Glassblowing and Death
Theft of Independence
Cookie Thief
Marble Thief
Book Thief
Art Thief

All books in 'An Introductory Series':
BIOLOGICAL PSYCHOLOGY 3RD EDITION
COGNITIVE PSYCHOLOGY THIRD EDITION
SOCIAL PSYCHOLOGY- 3RD EDITION
ABNORMAL PSYCHOLOGY 3RD EDITION
PSYCHOLOGY OF RELATIONSHIPS- 3RD EDITION
DEVELOPMENTAL PSYCHOLOGY 3RD EDITION
HEALTH PSYCHOLOGY
RESEARCH IN PSYCHOLOGY
A GUIDE TO MENTAL HEALTH AND TREATMENT AROUND THE WORLD- A GLOBAL LOOK AT DEPRESSION
FORENSIC PSYCHOLOGY
THE FORENSIC PSYCHOLOGY OF THEFT, BURGLARY AND OTHER CRIMES AGAINST PROPERTY
CRIMINAL PROFILING: A FORENSIC PSYCHOLOGY GUIDE TO FBI PROFILING AND GEOGRAPHICAL AND STATISTICAL PROFILING.
CLINICAL PSYCHOLOGY
FORMULATION IN PSYCHOTHERAPY
PERSONALITY PSYCHOLOGY AND INDIVIDUAL DIFFERENCES
CLINICAL PSYCHOLOGY REFLECTIONS VOLUME 1
CLINICAL PSYCHOLOGY REFLECTIONS VOLUME 2

THE RUSSIAN CASE

CULT PSYCHOLOGY
Police Psychology

www.ingramcontent.com/pod-product-compliance
Lightning Source LLC
LaVergne TN
LVHW012113070526
838202LV00056B/5715